IDA and BETTY
and the Secret Eggs

D1529887

IDA and BETTY
and the Secret Eggs

by Kay Chorao

CLARION BOOKS

New York

Watercolor, colored pencil and pen and ink
were used to create the full-color artwork.
The text type is ITC Novarese Book.

Clarion Books
a Houghton Mifflin Company imprint
215 Park Avenue South, New York, NY 10003
Text and Illustrations copyright © 1991 by Kay Chorao

Library of Congress Cataloging-in-Publication Data
Chorao, Kay.
Ida and Betty and the secret eggs / written and illustrated by Kay
Chorao.
p. cm.
Summary: Vacationing in the country, Ida, a spunky kitten, becomes
jealous when an older kitten makes friends with Ida's best friend,
Betty.
ISBN 0-395-52591-8
|1. Friendship—Fiction.   2. Country life—Fiction   3. Cats—
Fiction.| I. Title.
PZ7.C4463Icm   1991
|E|—dc20   90-43133
                                      CIP
                                      AC

H O R 10 9 8 7 6 5 4 3 2 1

To Betty

and in memory of a still-eggs summer

Ida couldn't wait. She couldn't wait to jump out of Mama's old bus, when it rattled into the yard of the house where she and brother Fred and Mama lived every summer. And she couldn't wait to run to Betty's house. Betty was Ida's best summer friend.

"Hey, Betty, it's me, Ida," yelled Ida when she got to Betty's yard.

"Shhhhhhh. In the tree," answered a soft voice.

Ida scrambled up the tree, past a chattering robin who hopped from branch to branch. She found Betty staring at a bird's nest.

"Look," whispered Betty.

Ida peered into the nest. There were four little blue eggs.

"A mama bird put them there yesterday," said Betty.

"Pretty," said Ida.

"Mmmmmm," said Betty, nodding up and down. "And someday they won't be eggs anymore. Baby birds are growing inside those eggs, and someday the babies will pop out."

"Wow," said Ida. "Like magic."

"They are our secret eggs," said Betty, climbing down out of the tree.

"Our secret," said Ida, following.

After that, Ida would telephone Betty every morning. She would call even before she ate breakfast.

"Are they still eggs?" she would ask, and Betty would answer, "Still eggs."

Mama would smile while she stirred the breakfast cereal. "You and the still eggs," she would say. And when Betty came to the door, Mama would hug her and call her "Still Eggs" and everyone would laugh, even Betty.

After breakfast, Ida and Betty would run to the tree and check the eggs again, just in case. Sometimes Mama Bird was sitting quietly on the nest. Sometimes she left the nest, so Ida and Betty could see the four little eggs, blue and perfect.

"Still eggs," Ida would whisper.

"Still eggs," Betty would answer.

Then they would climb down to the ground and race across the meadow. Grasshoppers whirred away in fright out of the tall grass.

Or they explored the woods, where Ida showed Betty thick grapevines, good for swinging.

Or they waded in the creek, where water tumbled over rocks, and where the crayfish darted into the shadows. Ida knew how to snatch the crayfish from their hiding places without hurting them. Betty knew how to make them dance in her lap, while she held their pinchers.

Sometimes Ida and Betty hid in Ida's barn. They jumped out at Fred when he came to find his comics, which he hid in the hayloft.

Then one day Lucinda appeared.

"Can I play?" she said.

"I guess so," said Ida. "Where are you from?"

"We are renting the red house down the road," said Lucinda, looking all around Ida's yard.

Ida wondered what Lucinda was looking for.

"Want to climb trees with us?" said Betty.

"No," said Lucinda. "I don't do that anymore."

"Want to catch crayfish?" said Ida.

"Ugh," said Lucinda.

"You pick then," said Ida.

"Let's dress up and put on a play," said Lucinda.

"I don't know," said Ida.

Lucinda went on. "I will be the magical queen. Betty will be the beautiful princess. And you will be the toad, Ida."

"I don't want to be the toad," grumbled Ida.

"Come on, Ida, dressing up is fun," said Betty.

"And your brother can be king," said Lucinda.

"Fred won't play," said Ida.

"Come on, Ida, let's dress up," said Betty. "We can use those clothes in your barn."

"Mama is giving away those old clothes," said Ida. "She told me not to touch them."

"If it's old stuff, no one will notice if we play a little with it," said Lucinda.

Then Lucinda grabbed Betty's paw and they raced to the barn.

"Hey, Betty, let's check the MAGIC EGGS!" yelled Ida.

Betty dropped Lucinda's paw and spun around. "You promised not to tell. That's our secret. You *promised*!" yelled Betty.

"I don't care," Ida yelled back.

Then Lucinda staggered out of the barn, balancing boxes on her head. They tumbled out of her paws and fell to the grass, scattering clothes and hats and shoes.

"She is just mad because you are prettier, and get to be the princess," said Lucinda.

"I am not," said Ida, stomping her foot. "I don't care at all."

"Ida, you broke a promise," said Betty.

"You can wear a princess dress and crown," said Lucinda, slipping an old blouse over Betty's head, and wrapping a belt around her ears. Then she pulled a little box from her pocket.

"Stars. You have stars!" said Betty, turning away from Ida. "I want stars on my ears and nose and tail and..."

"And I'm *going*," yelled Ida.

Lucinda was too busy rummaging through the clothes to answer.

Betty was too busy pasting on princess stars to answer.

So Ida left.

She climbed the tree in Betty's yard and startled Mama Bird, who flapped away. Ida peered into the nest.

"Still eggs," she whispered. But Betty wasn't there to say "Still eggs" back.

Tiny bits of sunshine flickered over the eggs, making them the softest glimmery blue Ida had ever seen. But Betty wasn't there to see, too.

"Goodbye, still eggs," Ida whispered, slipping out of the tree.

When Ida got home, Betty and Lucinda had disappeared, and Mama was mad.

"Clean up that mess in the yard right now," she said. "I told you not to get into those old clothes."

"But I didn't. It was Betty and that bossy Lucinda."

"Right now!" said Mama.

Ida ran to the yard and picked everything up.

Mama came and helped fold.

"Don't cry, Ida," said Mama. "I know you are sorry you made a mess with your friends."

"I didn't, and they aren't my friends. Betty doesn't like me. She likes Lucinda."

"Of course Betty likes you," said Mama, giving Ida a hug.

But that night Betty didn't come to play with Ida. So Ida caught lightning bugs alone.

And the next morning Ida didn't telephone Betty, and Betty didn't come over.

"No Still Eggs today?" asked Mama.

"No," said Ida, walking glumly out the door.

When Ida passed the barn, she heard voices. One was soft. The other was bossy loud.

"Betty and Lucinda are playing in *my* barn," said Ida.

The voices were coming from the hayloft, so Ida silently climbed the ladder and peeked over the edge of the loft. It was not Betty and Lucinda. It was Fred and Lucinda.

Ida held her breath and listened.

"So I sat on Betty's stomach until she *told*," said Lucinda.

"Told what?" said Fred.

"About her big magical secret. And you know what? It was just some silly bird eggs. Imagine, *bird* eggs."

Lucinda was balancing on the edge of Fred's milk carton, where Fred kept his comics.

"Mmmmmm," said Fred, turning a page.

"Anyway," Lucinda continued, "Betty cried and cried, just like a baby, because I made her tell about her old eggs."

"Betty's just a little kitten," said Fred, looking annoyed.

"I know. I only played with her and Ida so I could meet you. You are the only one around here who's my age. I can't stand playing with babies."

Hearing this, Ida stiffened with anger.

She noticed a rope tied to the milk carton. It was under the hay, just out of her reach. But quick as a flash Ida darted her paw out and grabbed the rope and pulled. The milk carton shot out from under Lucinda, who toppled headfirst into a pile of hay.

"That was mean, Fred," cried Lucinda. "You made me fall!"

"You just tripped over your own big feet," said Fred.

"My head hurts," howled Lucinda. "Boo hoo hoo!"

"Now who is a baby," said Fred.

Unseen, Ida scrambled down the ladder as fast as she could.

"Boo hoo hoo hoo!" she heard again as she ran out of the barn, into the morning sunlight. She didn't stop running until she rounded her house and bumped headlong into Betty.

"Hey," gasped Betty.

"Ooops, I'm sorry," said Ida.

"No, I'm sorry," said Betty. "I was just coming to tell you. I'm sorry I ran off with Lucinda."

"Here she comes," whispered Ida. "Let's hide."

So Betty and Ida scooted under a bush and watched Lucinda stomp past, out of Ida's yard. She was holding her head and howling.

"She only fell in the hay. That howling is all an act. She is just mad because Fred won't play with her," said Ida.

"She fell in the hay?" said Betty.

"Well, I sort of made her fall off Fred's box," said Ida, giggling.

"Good," said Betty, giggling too.

"Lucinda is mean. Do you know what she...?"

Then Ida stopped and looked at her good friend. "Never mind. Let's see if they are still eggs."

"Let's," said Betty.

So they ran to Betty's tree, climbed up, and looked into the nest.

The eggs were gone. In their place were four little birds with big bald heads and skinny little necks and great big beaks, wide open.

"Like magic," whispered Ida in wonder.

"Magic," whispered Betty.

Then the mama bird flew at them, so Ida and Betty tumbled back out of the tree. They fell in a heap at the bottom.

Laughing, they picked themselves up and ran through the tall grass, where grasshoppers whirred past their ears and the sunshine splashed all around.